RETOLD BY LISA TRUMBAUER
ILLUSTRATED BY AARON BLECHA

The Graphic Novel

THE THREE LITTLE PIGS

STONE ARCH BOOKS
MINNEAPOLIS   SAN DIEGO

Graphic Spin is published by Stone Arch Books
151 Good Counsel Drive, P.O. Box 669
Mankato, Minnesota 56002
www.stonearchbooks.com

Library of Congress Cataloging-in-Publication Data
Trumbauer, Lisa, 1963-
     The Three Little Pigs / by Lisa Trumbauer; illustrated by Aaron Blecha.
     p. cm. — (Graphic Spin)
     ISBN 978-1-4342-1195-8 (library binding)
     ISBN 978-1-4342-1395-2 (pbk.)
     1. Graphic novels. [1. Graphic novels. 2. Folkore. 3. Pigs—Folklore.] I. Blecha, Aaron, ill.
II. Three little pigs. English. III. Title.
PZ7.7.T78Th 2009
741.5'973—dc22   2008032050

Summary: When their mother sends them packing, the Three Little Pigs are forced to build
houses of their own. They better be sturdy and strong because the Big Bad Wolf is on the prowl,
and he's ready to huff and puff his way inside. Will they survive against this hungry beast? Or
will the pigs become his next tasty treat?

Creative Director: Heather Kindseth
Designer: Bob Lentz

1 2 3 4 5 6 14 13 12 11 10 09

Printed in the United States of America

THE **THIRD** LITTLE PIG

THE **SECOND** LITTLE PIG

CAST OF **CHARACTERS**

Long, long ago, at the edge of a village, lived a mother pig and her three sons.

Mama Pig took good care of her sons, and they enjoyed living at Mama's house.

But Mama Pig knew her sons were no longer little piglets.

My brothers don't know what they're talking about!

Straw makes a fine house.

It's light and easy for building.

Ah! A home of my own.

What's so hard about building your own house?

The next morning, the third Little Pig began to build his home.

It was...

...long...

...hard...

...work.

It took me all day, but it's finished!

A good day's work, and a strong, sturdy house to show for it.

The village where the Three Little Pigs lived was fairly safe.

Yet trouble lived in the nearby forest. Namely, the Big Bad Wolf.

The wolf didn't mean to be nasty. It was just his nature.

The next day ...

KNOCK
KNOCK

Little Pig, I was so rude yesterday. Let me make it up to you.

I know a place where some nice juicy turnips grow.

And where might that be?

At old Farmer Brown's just down the road.

I know the place. Would you like to meet tomorrow morning at six?

And where might that be?

Then let's meet tomorrow morning at five?

Tomorrow morning at five it is, my friend!

But the next morning . . .

BONK!

Now where is that Little Pig? Has he tricked me again?

I'll duck inside here. The wolf will never spot me.

Get out of my pot, you pig!

KLUNK!

Hey! You're paying for that!

Uh-oh! How do you stop this thing?

YEOW! Hot, hot, hot!

The Big Bad Wolf wasn't so bad anymore.

Now to find my brothers, if the Wolf has not eaten them already.

ABOUT THE AUTHOR

Lisa Trumbauer was the *New York Times* bestselling author of *A Practical Guide to Dragons*. In addition, she wrote about 300 other books for children, including mystery novels, picture books, and nonfiction books on just about every topic under the sun. (Including the sun!)

ABOUT THE ILLUSTRATOR

Aaron Blecha was raised by a school of slimy, yet gooey, giant squids in Green Bay, Wisconsin. Since then, Blecha has been working for ten years as an illustrator and designer with a hodgepodge of fun clients in the animation, publishing, toy, and entertainment industries. After many years in San Francisco, he now resides in London, where he is busy freelancing, avoiding crusty ghosts, and searching for the elusive Squidsquatch.

GLOSSARY

den (DEN)—home of a wild animal

kettle (KET-uhl)—a metal pot used for cooking

orchard (OR-churd)—a field or farm where fruit trees are grown

peddler (PED-lur)—someone who travels around selling things

rascal (RASS-kuhl)—someone who is mischievous or dishonest

rescue (RESS-kyoo)—to save someone who is in danger or trapped somewhere

sturdy (STUR-dee)—strong and firm

tricked (TRIKD)—fooled or cheated someone

turnip (TUR-nuhp)—a round, root vegetable

THE HISTORY OF THE

THREE LITTLE PIGS

Fairy tales are told in every corner of the world. No matter where they come from, there are similar elements in all fairy tales. There are almost always mythical characters, ranging from troublesome trolls to talking animals. Most fairy tales plot the "good" against the "evil," and many teach a lesson.

"The Three Little Pigs" has all of these features. Three house-building pigs battle against the sly wolf. In the end, the pig who took his time and built a proper home out of bricks is the only one to outsmart the wolf.

While the story of the three pigs has likely been around for centuries, it was not published until the 1800s. Writer Joseph Jacobs is credited with the most famous version of the tale. He published it in his collection, *English Fairy Tales,* in 1898. In this early version, the wolf eats the first and second pigs. In turn, the third pig boils up the wolf after he falls in the pot, then eats him for dinner.

Most early-published versions of the tale come from England. However, similar stories can be traced to other countries. "The Three Hares," a Turkish story, tells the tale of three rabbits and a fox. The first rabbit makes his home in a bush, only to be caught and eaten by the fox. The next rabbit tries out tree roots, but the fox eats him too. Finally, the third rabbit digs a long, deep burrow into the ground. Here he is safe from the fox, as well as from dogs and hunters.

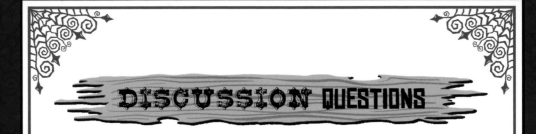

DISCUSSION QUESTIONS

1. Why do you think the first two brothers chose to build their homes with straw and sticks? Why do you think the third brother chose to build with bricks? What might this say about their characters?

2. The story says that the Big Bad Wolf doesn't mean to be nasty, but it was just in his nature. What does that mean? Can you think of other animals that behave a certain way because it is in their "nature"?

3. Each page of a graphic novel has several illustrations inside different panels. What is your favorite panel in this book? Describe what you like about the illustration and why it's your favorite.

WRITING PROMPTS

1. Imagine that the third little pig gets caught too. How could all three of the pigs escape the Big Bad Wolf? Write the getaway story.

2. Write your own version of "The Three Little Pigs," using different animals or even people as the characters. Who will be the hero in the story? Who will be the villain?

3. The wolf used turnips, apples, and the fair to tempt the third little pig out of his home. Pretend you are the little pig. What are three of your favorite things that the wolf might tempt you with?

INTERNET SITES

The book may be over, but the adventure is just beginning.

Do you want to read more about the subjects or ideas in this book? Want to play cool games or watch videos about the authors who write these books? Then go to FactHound. At www.facthound.com, you'll be able to do all that, and more. The FactHound website can also send you to other safe Internet sites.

Check it out!